D1348745

Tales of
Freedom

Tales of Freedom

Ben Okri

RIDER

LONDON · SYDNEY · AUCKLAND · JOHANNESBURG

3 5 7 9 10 8 6 4 2

Published in 2009 by Rider, an imprint of Ebury Publishing

Ebury Publishing is a division of the Random House Group

Copyright © 2009 Ben Okri

The Random House Group Limited Reg. No. 954009

Addresses for companies within the Random House Group
can be found at www.rbooks.co.uk

A CIP catalogue record for this book
is available from the British Library

The Random House Group Limited supports The Forest Stewardship
Council (FSC), the leading international forest certification organisation.
All our titles that are printed on Greenpeace approved FSC certified paper
carry the FSC logo. Our paper procurement policy can be found at
www.rbooks.co.uk/environment

Mixed Sources
Product group from well-managed
forests and other controlled sources
www.fsc.org   Cert no. TT-COC-2139
© 1996 Forest Stewardship Council

Printed and bound in Great Britain by CPI Mackays, Chatham ME5 8TD

ISBN 978-1-8460-4157-0 (hardback)
ISBN 978-1-8460-4158-7 (paperback)

Contents

Acknowledgements

Material in this collection has been previously broadcast or first published as follows:

'Belonging' first broadcast by the BBC and published in *Ode* Magazine; 'The Mysterious Anxiety of Them and Us' first broadcast by the BBC and published in *Global Report*; 'Music for a Ruined City' published by *Ode* Magazine; 'The Racial Colourist' published in *VSO* Magazine; 'The Black Russian' published in *Diaspora City* (Arcadia Books, 2003); 'Wild Bulls' published in *The London Magazine*; 'The Golden Inferno' published in *Ode* Magazine; 'The Secret Castle' first broadcast by the BBC; and 'The War Healer' published in *The Spectator*.

The Comic
Destiny

Book One

One

Old Man and Old Woman sat in the forest. Pinprop sat at their feet. They were in a clearing. They listened to footsteps running in their direction, and to a siren wailing in the distance. After a while the footsteps receded.

Old Man and Old Woman were silent. They sat behind a table. Pinprop sat in front. Every now and again Pinprop looked to the left and then to the right. He put his ear to the ground. He grinned.

Suddenly, Old Man, with dignity, said: 'YES.'

Old Woman looked at him. Then she too said:

'Yes.'

There was a long silence. Not even the wind could be heard. Old Man kicked Pinprop beneath the table and, sternly, said:

'Pinprop!'

Pinprop sat up straight and came to his senses.

'Oh, sir,' he said. 'Definitely yes. Indeed, sir. A big yes.'

'Good. Good,' Old Man said.

Two

Pinprop leapt up from his cross-legged position as if inspired. He paced up and down the clearing, in front of the table. He stopped, and laughed. Then he performed a dance step, turned grim, and laughed again. Without turning to face the old couple, he said:

'As we were saying. We have indeed found the spot, and the spot has indeed found us. We have not yet arrived, but every point at which we stop requires a re-definition of our destination.'

'You mean we have not yet arrived?' said Old Woman, with a tone of indignation.

'Oh, yes,' replied Pinprop. 'But only tentatively.'

'What!' Old Woman cried.

'It's like this,' said Pinprop reassuringly. 'Every time a goose lays an egg it implies many more eggs to be laid. Every time a trap catches a mouse there is an intimation of many more mice to be caught. The final destination of the goose is when it can become an egg; and with the trap it is when it ends up as a mouse.'

'Yes,' Old Woman said. 'That makes a lot of sense. Go on.'

Pinprop resumed pacing. He appeared slightly confused.

'I'm glad it makes sense.'

'Well, go on.'

'Well, em, where was I?'

'The mouse becomes a trap,' Old Woman said, irritated.

'Yes. Where was I before that?'

'You were here, you fool,' Old Man snapped.

'That's right,' said Pinprop. 'How easily I forget. Well, now that we have arrived temporarily, we must pay our tributes to where we are.'

Three

Pinprop became silent. Then he looked around wildly. There was a touch of terror on his face.

'Where are we?' he asked.

'Pinprop, will you stop this,' Old Woman said, exasperated. 'You were just going to tell us that.'

'No, madam,' replied Pinprop. 'I was simply going to remind us what brought us here.'

'And what is that?' Old Woman asked, with some interest.

'Well, em, do you want me to be honest?'

'No, definitely not, Pinprop,' Old Man said, 'You know how much we hate honesty.'

'That's what I thought.'

'Well?' pressed Old Woman.

'Well then,' said Pinprop blithely, 'we came here because we were looking for somewhere else to go.'

'That is disconcertingly too near the truth,' said Old Man.

'Well then, we came here because we were tired.'

'Still too near the truth.'

'We came in search of violence?'

'Too near.'

'Looking for a place to die?'

'PINPROP!!!' Old Man cried.

'Forgive me, sir. It simply slipped out.'

'Well then, rectify it.'

'Definitely, sir.'

'Don't use that word "definite".'

'Why not, sir?'

'Blasphemy!'

'Alright, sir.'

'Then why?' asked Old Woman. 'Why? Why? Why, Pinprop?'

'Yes, why? Emmmm. Can I be verbose about it?'

'Certainly,' said Old Man.

'Ugliness,' began Pinprop, 'and the cruelty of myth. The excessive stench of putrefying bodies. Too much blood and tiredness, and iron in the throat. Small places turning septic, and large spaces tumbling into confusion. And people becoming hell. And hunger bloating too many bellies.

Tiredness and tiredness and chaos. And fear, Sir, limitless fear.'

'You should be hanged, Pinprop,' snarled Old Man.

'Too much neurosis and disease and new diseases.'

'You should be flagellated, Pinprop,' snarled Old Woman.

'And the shrinking of cages till we can no longer fly.'

'You should be served for dinner,' Old Man cried.

'And squabbles and lies and terror. Self-destruction and the wilful destruction of other people. And sickness, sir, sickness in the throat and stomach and food and streets and faces and the air ...'

Cutting through his iteration, Old Man and Old Woman shouted as one:

'The chain, Pinprop, the chain of iron and blood.'

'Oh, yes,' said Pinprop, a little chastened. 'I forgot. I got carried away.'

With a noticeable change in their voices, and still speaking as one:

'Yes, Pinprop, you got carried away.'

'What?' he enquired, puzzled.

'Yes!'

'Oh, indeed, yes,' said Pinprop, relieved. 'Yes very very much. A fat yes to everything.'

He laughed. He seemed pleased with himself. He did a dance step.

'Yes, Pinprop. Yes,' they both said, with a decidedly sinister tone.

Four

Then, quite suddenly, Old Man and Old Woman kicked away their chairs and tossed aside the table. And while Pinprop danced unsuspectingly they grabbed him and, with surprising ease, lifted him up and carried him off into the woods. They dumped him on the ground with a thud. Pinprop wailed and laughed wildly at the same time, while they chained him. Then, wheezing and coughing, Old Man and Old Woman returned to the clearing.

Breathing heavily, Old Man said:

'That was a job well done.'

'A satisfactory achievement,' Old Woman replied.

'A major victory, considering our ages.'

'Let us not talk about age.'

'I'm exhausted.'

'Do you think we were a bit too hard on him?'

'Definitely,' said Old Man, with dignity.

'That's wonderful.'

They picked up the chairs, put the table back in its former place, and resumed their seats.

'Now all we can do is wait,' Old Woman said.

'Yes.'

'And the boredom?'

'Oh, that. Let's enjoy that as well.'

'Ah, yes.'

'Yes to all that.'

'Yes to everything.'

'And to nothing.'

Five

There was a brief silence. Then Old Man and Old Woman began to reminisce, to speak as if the other weren't there. They spoke aloud, to themselves, in that clearing, in the forest, beneath an indeterminate sky. They spoke alternately, as if they were in a dream, or a trance, or a ritual. Old Woman spoke first.

'I remember all those signs on the trees on our way here . . .'

Then Old Man spoke:

'I forget to remember but I certainly recollect the skeletons that strange tribe built their houses with . . .'

Old Woman, interrupting, said:

'And I remember that the signs formed an interminable sentence. If you miss out a tree or get to the wrong one first the whole sentence gets jumbled up.'

Old Man continued the thread of his reminiscences:

'The skeletons were polished and left intact. The bones were decorated. The hollows in the skulls were stuffed with amusing artefacts. The tribe thought it had finally arrived and then one night in history the owners of the skeletons turned up and began to remove their bones and skulls. The buildings collapsed, and only the artefacts remained.'

Old Woman, increasingly mesmerised by her reminiscence, spoke with some urgency:

'I remember that I had to keep rearranging the sentences in my head. At first they seemed like nonsense, a pointless word puzzle. I was fascinated with this elaborate rubbish till I realised that I was in fact reading the story of my life that had been scattered all over the place.'

They were each lost in their separate monologues. They picked up the thread of their reminiscences as if they were sleepwalkers in an obscure theatre of the mind. With increasing intensity, Old Man continued:

'The strange tribe had built an unhealthy routine around the skeletons. They didn't realise that the skeletons were alive and subversive. And so their routines became hellish and the people became afflicted with diseases that only a final destruction could cure. I mean, it was funny and sad to see them living their daily lives, trying to unwind the intricate confusion of so many threads forever entangled. It was even funnier when . . .'

And Old Woman, in the voice of a bizarre tropical bird, swooped down into her extended act of memory.

'I was horrified but I laughed and said to Pinprop "There must be a place out there". And whenever I could I either tore down the signs or rewrote them. It was ugly seeing intimate details of my life on those trees, things like when I had my first period and all the satisfaction I derived from inflicting revenge on someone who had insulted me in some small way. It was all so banal. I rewrote them, indeed I did. And . . .'

Plunging deeper into his mood, Old Man said:

'. . . a man came along and saw his skeleton embedded in the body of a building. He struggled so hard to get it out that he extricated the skeleton but ended up part of the building himself. Afterwards the building became empty because they thought it was spooked and for several centuries the man was howling away in an empty house with no-one around to be terrified. And . . .'

Old Woman laughed lightly to herself at her memories.

'. . . I thought it was funny myself that I had rewritten the last sign I saw that said "And I was lost". I simply made it read: "And I took up a room in a hotel and lived there ever after." I like happy endings, you see.'

Then she turned serious.

'No-one can blame me for being angry, therefore, when Pinprop came back and told me that we were lost. I asked him how he knew and the fool said: "Well, em, I read it on a tree".'

Six

At that moment Pinprop began howling from the woods. He howled like one in a nightmare.

'And boredom, sir and madam,' he cried. 'What shall we do about hunger? What are we to do about violence, I ask you?'

'Tell the fool to shut up,' snapped Old Man.

'Shut up, Pinprop!' Old Woman barked.

'But if I shut up, sir, who would hear me?'

'No-one wants to hear you, Pinprop,' Old Man said.

'Then I shall speak to myself.'

'Then we shall listen,' replied Old Man.

'That's fine by me,' came the obstinate Pinprop. 'I am bored. I am tired. I shall sing a song. I am afraid of being bored so I shall make love instead. I shall make love to these chains and I shall do it so much that the chains will float and we will all have to swim.'

'Empty threats, Pinprop.'

'Tell him to shut up. I don't want to be accidentally impregnated by a eunuch.'

'Surely, you're too old for that.'

'I shall outdo the rainstorms, sir,' Pinprop shouted. 'Who knows what clouds are anyway?'

'Shut up, Pinprop.'

'I was merely expressing a fantasy.'

'Your fantasy makes us sick,' said Old Woman.

'I was merely trying to nauseate you into freeing me from these rusted chains,' cried Pinprop, beating the chains on the ground.

'You'd better release him.'

'And what will be his price for freedom?' Old Man asked, wearily.

'Obedience,' said Old Woman.

Seven

Old Man got up reluctantly. He trundled into the woods, and soon returned with Pinprop trailing behind him, limply. Old Man sat in his chair. Pinprop took up his customary position in front of the table. The sky had darkened a little over the clearing.

'Now we shall have some peace,' Old Woman said.

'I was trying to forget something,' muttered Old Man, 'but instead I remembered.'

'I was trying to remember something,' mumbled Old Woman, 'but now I've forgotten.'

Pinprop, almost in a whisper, said:

'A bloated NO to all this, and a monstrous NO to all that iron.'

The sky improved. Then Old Man, with dignity, said:

'Now for some boredom.'

Old Woman, also with dignity:

'Now for some lies.'

'And now,' said Pinprop, 'that we have arrived at a temporary destination . . .'

'A proper yes,' said Old Man.

'A resonant yes,' said Old Woman.

'. . . I may as well remember for myself . . .' Pinprop continued.

'The vote is taken,' Old Man said.

'And silence wins,' Old Woman said.

'. . . that there are many sad people . . .' Pinprop went on.

'A deafening victory for silence,' said Old Woman.

'A violent victory for silence,' said Old Man.

'. . . who would never arrive . . .' said Pinprop.

'Because silence stands for lies,' Old Woman said.

'And lies stand for victory,' Old Man said.

'. . . because there is nowhere to arrive at . . .' continued Pinprop.

'And victory stands for banality.'

'And banality represents happiness.'

'. . . and travelling is the only place there is . . .' said Pinprop.

'Look well, therefore, at the trap,' intoned Old Man.

'And regard carefully the mouse,' cried Old Woman.

'. . . and arriving is the best cliché to feed to skeletons,' concluded Pinprop.

'A resounding yes to arrivals,' bellowed the old man.

'A sonorous yes to escapes,' crowed the old woman.

There was a brief silence. Old Man and Old Woman looked sternly at Pinprop. Old Woman kicked him beneath the table. Pinprop giggled. Then he stopped. Then, in a demonic whisper, he said:

'A still, small defiant NO to all that.'

Then they were perfectly immobile, as at the completion of an ancient ritual.

Book Two

One

It is not possible to say whether time had passed. Old Man and Old Woman were asleep on the table. Pinprop sat on the ground in front of them, nodding and trying to stay awake. Then there came the sound of foot-steps running in their direction; and in the distance the wailing of a siren.

Now and then Old Woman clapped her hands together, and went back to sleep. Old Man snored.

The footsteps got closer. Then there was the noise of exhausted breathing in the woods nearby. Then finally a Man staggered into the clearing. He stopped, saw Pinprop, and sighed.

'Thank goodness,' he said.

Then he collapsed on the ground.

Two

Old Man raised his head, saw the Man, and went back to sleep. Old Woman lifted her head, saw the Man, clapped her hands together, inspected her palms, and flicked something away with her finger. Then she went back to sleep. Pinprop raised his head, regarded the Man, and resumed nodding in and out of sleep.

After a while the Man got up, dusted himself, and looked about him. He looked from left to right, and back again. He saw Pinprop sitting cross-legged, and went over, and prodded him.

'Hello, excuse me, please,' he said.

Pinprop looked up at him, and fell back to nodding.

'Excuse me, please.'

Pinprop regarded him again, and pushed him away.

'What's the matter with you?' the Man said. 'All I want is to ask a question.'

Pinprop made an angry face at him.

'Oh, I see,' the Man said. 'You're dumb. That's alright then.'

Pinprop resumed nodding. The Man went on talking.

'It's just that I've been running for a long time. Did you hear all that noise?'

Pinprop nodded.

'They've been chasing me,' the Man continued. 'I've never been so tired in all my life. I've never been more terrified either. Do you know that feeling, when it's as if you would be running for the rest of your life and you would be pursued by a kind of demonic force? I mean, it all kind of happened naturally. Do you understand what I'm trying to say?'

Pinprop nodded.

'It's nice to know someone understands.'

Pinprop snored. The Man went on.

'I mean, all this time I've been running I never saw a single soul. Only trees and sand and water. Especially water. I could never wash myself in it, nor could I drink of it. I was too busy fleeing, you see. Do you understand what I mean?'

Pinprop remained perfectly still.

'You don't. That's alright,' the Man said. 'I always had problems getting people to understand me. My headmaster used to say I was a natural victim and so no matter how well I expressed myself I would always be misunderstood. So you see, I don't even know how long I've been running. It's strange, you know, because even when it was a matter of freedom, life and death, I kept having guilt feelings about stupid things like how I smelt and whether my armpits or my crotch stank. Do you think I smell? I mean can you smell me?'

Pinprop nodded vigorously.

'So I was right, then.'

Pinprop didn't move.

'It was like that at the asylum. Water, trees, sand. On and on. I could never touch them. They were just there. It got too much, you see. I saw them so intensely that they took on an extraordinary quality of beauty. I never saw human beings or animals. Just those things. Then one day I knew I had to escape.'

Three

The Man began pacing the clearing.

'I don't want you to get the wrong idea. It wasn't a dramatic sort of asylum, with people going about like zombies and foaming at the mouth and all that. It was a place for mild cases. But it was all a lie. I saw one of the inmates bash in another person's head. And do you know why?'

Old Woman clapped her hands together. Old Man sneezed. Pinprop pulled his nose, slapped his thigh, and resumed nodding. The Man went on.

'Well, it was because the inmate did not like the way the other fellow sniffed. It was like this, you see. They sort of shared a room. The man who had his head bashed in sniffed far too much for his own good. The other fellow complained for ages that he wanted another room. He never got another room. So one day they had an argument and the fellow who sniffed a lot sniffed and sniffed and sniffed. He went on for hours. At night, at noon, at breakfast, he did it wherever the other fellow was. We found him one morning. His head was like an orange mauled by a gorilla. It was all hushed up, you see. The chap had a decent funeral.'

Silence.

'Don't you find that funny?'

Pinprop slapped his thigh.

'Oh well, I do,' said the Man. 'I find almost everything I remember sort of funny. And when I find things funny I don't laugh. I cry. If you tell me a joke and it's a good one I could cry for hours. That's why I don't listen to jokes.'

Four

The Man paused. He stared at Pinprop contemplatively, and then carried on.

'You know, I saw a good joke while I was running. It sort of wore thin after a while, though. The trees had signs on them, the same sign. Do you know what it read?'

Pinprop sneezed.

'It read: "Room to Let". And all the signs were different. Some were small, some were big, some were colourful and so on. The best one I saw was carved on the tree trunk and then painted blue and yellow. It made the room feel like a really special room.'

He paused, and then went on.

'I used to have a good room once. Then it went sour. You know, routines and routines. I used to live with a brother. He was filthy and I was clean. I would spend hours arranging and rearranging the place. We had lots of horrible arguments. You know, about every silly thing. We fought a lot and he always beat me up. Like a child. Do you want to know a secret?'

Pinprop remained still.

'Well, I'll tell you anyway. Since you are dumb you can't tell anybody, can you? Well, the secret is that I killed him.'

Pinprop nodded.

'Doesn't that surprise you?' the Man asked, a little baffled. 'Isn't it a little hair-raising?'

Pinprop was still.

'That's alright then. You've probably murdered someone yourself. Anyway, I killed him. It wasn't particularly difficult. I simply smashed his head with a hammer.'

The Man laughed. It was long and perfectly normal laughter. He fell silent. Then:

'After that it was the asylum. And then running. And then you.'

Five

There was a long silence, during which the Man studied Pinprop. Then he looked around him, at the clearing, the woods, the sky. He walked round the immobile Pinprop.

'How strange!' he said. 'I've been talking to myself all this time. I'm not even dreaming. What a bad impression you must have of me. Do you have a bad impression of me?'

Pinprop remained immobile.

'Do you?'

Pinprop didn't move.

The Man proceeded to shake Pinprop, who did not wake. Then he kicked Pinprop.

'Are you dead or alive?'

Pinprop groaned sleepily, and nodded.

'This is driving me mad,' the Man cried.

He kicked Pinprop a few more times. Pinprop sneezed, but remained still.

'Not again, oh no, not again,' the Man shouted.

Striding about the clearing, stamping his feet, and pulling his hair, he worked himself into a frenzy. Then he suddenly stopped. A weird calm came over him.

'Oh, yes. Yes, indeed. It won't be my fault, yes,' he said.

Then he laughed, looked excitedly about the clearing, ran off into the woods, and soon came back with a thick tree-branch in his hand.

Six

As the Man got to the middle of the clearing Pinprop yawned, stretched, looked up at him, and said:

'Oh, hello. You've recovered, have you?'

The Man stuttered, at a loss.

'Good,' said Pinprop. 'Definitely good.'

'Ah, yes,' replied the Man, perplexed.

'You do look a bit agitated,' said Pinprop, pointedly. 'Are you alright?'

'Yes, indeed,' the Man answered, looking awkwardly at the thick piece of wood in his hands, which he dropped. 'Em, I was just going to make a fire. It is a bit cold.'

'Good,' said Pinprop. 'Definitely so.'

There was a brief silence.

'You mean you were really asleep all that time?' the Man asked.

'As asleep as sleep is possible,' Pinprop replied, nonchalantly. 'That is if you take into consideration the amount of sleep that is not possible. Why?'

'Well, you see, I was under the impression that you were dumb.'

'Dumb?' said Pinprop, laughing. 'I've been called many things but not dumb.'

'Well, I was talking to you.'

'Oh. What about?'

Flustered, the Man said:

'About life, my job, my wife and all that.'

'You mean boredom, of course.'

'Yes, boredom.'

'A profound subject boredom is.'

'Very much so.'

Seven

There was another long silence. Old Woman clapped her hands together. Old Man woke up. He sat bolt upright, staring straight ahead of him, as if deep in thought, or in a daze. Then after a while he woke up Old Woman.

Pinprop, addressing the Man, said:

'Was anybody else here?'

'No.'

'I must have dreamt that someone was kicking me.'

Laughing nervously, the Man said:

'I only brushed past you a number of times.'

'That explains it,' said Pinprop, dryly.

'Things are magnified in dreams, you know.'

'Yes, definitely.'

'Do you know where I can find that room advertised on the trees?' the Man asked, in a new voice.

'Room? What room?'

'It's just a room,' said the Man, defensively. 'Didn't you see the signs on the trees?'

'No.'

'That's alright then. Forget the subject. It's not important anyway.'

'Isn't it?'

'No. Why should it be?'

'You were right. Let's forget the subject.'

'A fine idea.'

They were silent for a while.

'What's your name?' the Man asked suddenly.

'My name?'

'Yes.'

'Mada.'

'A nice short name.'

'And what's yours?'

'It's not important.'

'Yes. Definitely.'

'And what are you doing here?'

'Me?'

'Yes.'

'Oh, I'm, em, tired,' said Pinprop, blithely. 'I'm impotent.'

'I see. How interesting.'

'And you?'

'No. I'm not impotent,' said the Man.

'How do you know?'

'What?'

'I said, good. But what are you doing here?'

'It's not really important, if you see what I mean.'

'Certainly.'

They were silent again. The Man stared into the forest, blankly.

Eight

'I see that the tribe has caught up with us,' said Old Man.

'Skeletons, I think,' said Old Woman.

'A harmless liar,' said Pinprop.

'Are you talking to me?' asked the Man.

'No.'

'Harmless?' wondered Old Man.

'Harmful,' said Old Woman.

'A hyena, I suspect,' said Pinprop.

'A hyena? Where?' asked the Man.

'In the distance,' replied Pinprop. 'Beside me.'

'Beside you?' said the Man.

'Shut up,' said Pinprop.

'What about your so-called tributes, Pinprop?' piped Old Woman.

'And temporary arrivals?' added Old Man.

'Hollow. A sham,' replied Pinprop.

'Are you referring to me by any chance?' the Man asked, with a tinge of menace.

'I said shut up.'

'Are we going or are we to listen to this fool?' demanded Old Woman.

'You can be verbose if you like, Pinprop.'

'If you tell me to shut up again . . .' began the Man.

'Isolate him!' cried Old Woman.

'. . . I will most certainly . . .' continued the Man.

'Chain him!' said Old Man.

'. . . crack your head,' bellowed the Man.

'A statement of iron,' said Old Woman.

'Definitely of rust,' chimed Old Man.

'Did you hear me?' cried the Man.

'Gut-rot,' said Pinprop.

'What?'

'The vote is taken,' said Old Woman.

'And violence wins,' said Old Man.

'A definite victory to isolation,' proclaimed Pinprop.

'Are you mad?' asked the Man, baffled.

Old Man and Old Woman rose from their seats.

'Slave!' said Old Man.

'Sir!'

'The table and chairs,' said Old Woman.

'I said are you mad?'

'A throaty yes to new arrivals,' declared Old Man, as he left the clearing.

'A warm yes to new journeys,' Old Woman intoned, following him.

'A solid yes to all that,' said Pinprop, carrying the table and chairs.

Soon all three of them had vanished into the forest.

The Man stood alone in the clearing.

'Insane. Insane. This is madness,' he said.

There was complete silence.

'I've got to find that room,' he said, after a while.

He sat down on the ground.

'Yes.'

Then, after a moment, there came the wail of the siren in the distance, coming closer.

'Heavens! Not again!' he cried.

Then, agitated, he jumped up. He ran off into the forest in the direction from which he had originally come. Then he ran back, across the clearing, in the opposite direction.

Book Three

One

In another clearing, in the forest, a young man and a young woman sat at a distance from one another. They were surrounded by a dense screen of trees and shrubs. There were muted bird calls in the air, and the faint noise of a baby crying. On a tree there was a sign which read 'Eden to Let'.

The young man and young woman, with their hands outstretched on the ground, barely touched one another. The sky was clear.

'I wish you wouldn't be so cruel to me,' said the young man.

'I'm not being cruel to you,' replied the young woman.

'Yes you are.'

'No I'm not.'

'Do we have to argue again?'

'Yes.'

'Why do we have to argue and argue?'

'I don't know,' said the young woman. 'I suppose it's the most important part of our relationship.'

'No it's not.'

'Stop telling me what is and what isn't.'

'I'm not telling you anything. I'm just disagreeing, that's all.'

'Well, stop that as well.'

'We don't have to go on like this, you know.'

'Why not?'

'Because we are married. Much more than that, we have been together for a long time and we should have reached a deep understanding by now.'

'Well, haven't we?'

'I don't know,' said the young man. 'It's just that we argue and fight and hurt each other so much.'

'And don't you find any satisfaction in that?'

The young man smiled with pleasure, and then said:

'I can't say that I don't.'

'Then what are you blathering about?'

'It's just that, you see, we are here all by ourselves. There's nobody else around. We have no need to pretend that we don't get on with one another. You know how people used to envy us our passion and how, because of that, they used to spoil things for us, and how, because of that, we had to disguise our feelings. Well, now that we've been wandering about together there is no need for all that. I mean, I really want to discover you again.'

'God, you're a moaner,' said the young woman.

'Why do you say that?'

'Well, for the past many years we've been discovering each other again and again. After a fight we discover each other. After you've gone away to live with someone else and you've run back, we've discovered each other. After I had the baby we discovered each other again. Don't you get tired of these discoveries?'

'No, I think discoveries are wonderful.'

'You mean like discovering our capacity for cruelty?'

'That as well.'

'And discovering our insecurities?'

'Yes. Yes.'

'And that it is our cruelty and weaknesses that bind us together?'

'Yes. Wonderful symbiosis.'

'And secretly discovering how much we hate each other's strengths and beauties?'

'It's all part of it.'

'And that we've made a tolerable hell for each other?'

'A tolerable hell is better than an impossible heaven.'

'You are a fool,' said the young woman.

'So I am.'

'But I love you.'

'I love you too.'

'I feel a lot of tenderness for you.'

'I feel a volcanic warmth for you.'

'You seducer.'

'You . . . I don't know what.'

'Do you love me?'

'Do you promise,' said the young man, 'that if I answer honestly we won't get into another argument?'

'Yes. I just want to know.'

'Well then, yes. You know I do. We wouldn't have stayed together all this time if I didn't.'

'You stupid fool!' cried the young woman.

'What?'

'I said you stupid fool.'

'What did I say wrong?'

'You know perfectly well why we've stayed together all this time.'

'I know,' said the young man, perplexed. 'I've just said it.'

'You bloody moron.'

'Look, I'm sorry if I didn't say it with enough tenderness.'

'Who cares about your idiotic tenderness?'

'It's just that I thought you'd be bored by it.'

'We stayed together precisely because we did not really love each other.'

'I admit there's an element of that.'

'We simply wanted to love one another, didn't we?'

'Yes. Correct,' the young man said, brightly. 'The want precedes the process.'

'You idiot. I mean we desperately wanted to be in love with something or other. We were lonely people. It seemed more sensible to fall in love with another person who also wanted to fall in love, than to love a chair or a cat or an idea.'

'Correct again. The process then invents itself.'

'We knew all along that what other people thought was love was really a well-organised routine on our parts. An intricate pattern of tolerance and organisation. A relationship.'

'You can't say we haven't had a good life together. All those holidays, visits, our jobs, Christmases, surprises, ups and downs, the new house that we bought.'

'And the baby.'

'Yes, the baby. That was special, wasn't it?'

'Yes. It was very special. I hated having it.'

'No you didn't. Do you remember what you said at the time?'

'I think I groaned madly all the time.'

'I mean afterwards.'

'I said it was nice to have that load off my belly.'

'No. Not then. Stop being facetious about an important experience in our lives.'

'Speak for yourself.'

'Okay, I'll tell you what you said.'

'Go on, then.'

Two

As he spoke his face became radiant. His gestures became more expressive. For a moment he was transfigured in the strange light of the clearing.

'You said that while you were having the baby it felt as if you were creating new spaces in the universe. You felt that as you pushed and pushed you were pushing the universe, moving it, opening up new worlds, expanding the miraculous spaces. You said you felt like God.'

'I couldn't have said that. It was a horrible experience. I couldn't move for days.'

'That's why God had a rest on Sunday.'

There was silence.

'You are so naive,' the young woman said, gently, 'and yet I love you.'

'I love you too.'

'There you go again, idiot. Always parroting me.'

'I'm not parroting you.'

'Then why do you say you love me?'

'Because I do.'

'What is love, then?'

'That's a difficult question,' said the young man, taken aback. 'The only way to tackle a question like this is to be honest. Love is what two people feel. An attraction. Something wonderful. It sort of gets you here.'

He dramatically placed his hands over his heart.

'You mean,' said the young woman, coolly, 'like a heart attack?'

'No. Look, let's not get into this.'

'Why not? I've got to understand what you mean.'

'It's a feeling, you see,' said the young man, struggling. 'A great feeling. When you see the one you love you sort of tremble, your throat feels dry, your hands become clumsy, you . . . all that.'

'I think you are trying to describe a seizure.'

'Look, didn't you ever feel anything like that for me in the beginning?'

'No.'

'But you said you did.'

'I only shook a bit and blew my nose a lot.'

'Those are symptoms.'

'I had a cold, remember.'

'You even shed a few tears.'

'Dust in my eyes.'

'When we were together, really, for the first time, I was proud to note that you wept.'

'You had a habit of scratching me,' said the young woman. 'I couldn't bear it and I couldn't bear to tell you.'

'You never loved me then.'

'I did. In a different way.'

'I suppose you did,' said the young man, crestfallen.

'Look, stop behaving like a baby. Come closer to me. We haven't touched one another for a long time. Come on, come closer to me.'

'Are you sure?'

'Of course I am.'

'That would be so wonderful.'

'Come on, then.'

The young man smiled, and moved farther away from her.

'That's better,' the young woman said. 'You feel so warm. I can take you better like this. Come a bit closer still.'

'This is really lovely,' said the young man. 'You feel soft and velvety.'

He moved farther away from her.

'You know this is why I was against us having separate bedrooms. Touch can be a profound experience,' the young man said.

'It should be.'

'It's pure electricity.'

'Magic.'

'Wonder.'

'Let's lie down together and just enjoy each other in silence.'

They lay down, and mimed being close together. They behaved as if they were touching each other, with great feeling and delight.

Three

Then, after some time, in a gentle voice, the young man said:

'It would be nice to find a room.'

'Yes,' replied the young woman, 'I've been dreaming about that ever since we got lost.'

'You know, a nice cosy room where we would have no arguments, no jealousies, no routines, no boredom, no fights.'

'Yes. No jobs, no poverty, no diseases.'

'Don't talk about diseases,' the young man said, with a hint of fear.

'I'm sorry, I forgot.'

'Yes. No ideologies. No need to conform.'

'And no loneliness and fear and insecurity.'

'A room where we can go on creating beautiful spaces and expanding the universe.'

'Yes. Really pushing it all back and making it all real with our vitality,' said the young woman.

'There would be no networks, no shrinking of self.'

'And certainly no skeletons.'

'Neither in the cupboard, nor outside it.'

'Wouldn't it be nice,' said the young woman tenderly, 'to have the baby there with us?'

'Yes.'

'It's a shame, though.'

'Yes.'

'Do you suppose,' wondered the young woman, 'that such a room exists?'

'No. But it's worth dreaming about.'

'If it doesn't exist I'll settle for any old room. I feel tired.'

'So do I,' said the young man. 'But let's not talk about tiredness.'

'Yes. I forgot again.'

'There's too much to escape from.'

'And nowhere to escape to.'

Four

They were silent and then, suddenly, in a burst, they began speaking again, with urgency.

'I can't bear it,' said the young man.

'Neither can I.'

'I'm tired.'

'I'm ill.'

'I'm hungry.'

'I'm sick of everything.'

'My head hurts again.'

'So does mine.'

'It really hurts.'

'I think I'm going to scream,' said the young woman.

'I'm going to cry.'

'I don't think I can move.'

'Neither can I.'

'I wish somebody would help us.'

'I can't bear it.'

'I'm afraid.'

'I'm terrified.'

'I think we are alone.'

'I've always been afraid of that.'

'Are you there?'

'Yes,' said the young man. 'Are you?'

'Yes.'

'Let's hold each other.'

'Yes.'

They stretched out their hands. The tips of their fingers barely touched one another. There was silence.

'Are you there?' the young man asked.

'Yes. Are you?'

'Yes.'

'I'm still afraid.'

Then, from the surrounding forest, the sound of bird calls intensified momentarily.

'Those birds sound strange,' the young man said.

'I can't hear them.'

There was another silence.

'Are you there?'

'Yes.'

'This silence frightens me,' said the young man. 'Say something. Anything.'

After a long pause, the young woman said:

'This could be the best moment of our lives.'

* * *

There was another stretch of silence.

'I'm afraid,' said the young woman, after a while.

'So am I.'

'I wish someone would come along.'

'So do I.'

Five

In the depths of the silence there was a faint trace of music. Pinprop emerged from the woods, into the clearing, with the table and chairs balanced in a compact form on his head. He stopped in the middle of the clearing and contemplated the young couple lying on the ground. Soon Old Man and Old Woman also appeared from the woods.

'This seems an ideal spot,' said Old Man.

'Our destination is the only ideal spot,' said Pinprop.

'This seems a stained ideal spot,' said Old Woman.

'Do you think we should drive them away?' Old Man said, indicating the young couple, who did not notice the new presences.

'The place where hyenas sleep is not ideal for the lion,' intoned Old Woman.

'If I may be verbose,' said Pinprop, 'I'd like to say that these precincts have been defiled with gloom. We should proceed, sir and madam, to where there is no confusion.'

'No skeletons,' said Old Man.

'No repetitions,' said Old Woman.

'No trees, sand or water.'

'No words.'

'What do you say, sir and madam?' asked Pinprop.

'I am tired. I can barely walk,' said Old Woman.

'My life is draining out of me,' said Old Man.

'People never really die before they have arrived ideally, sir and madam,' observed Pinprop.

'We are too old to chase ideals,' said Old Woman.

'We are too old to seek new beginnings,' said Old Man.

Then they fell into their ritual of remembrance again, speaking without hearing the other; interrupting, overlapping, in their inward speech outwardly spoken. Old Woman began.

'I remember on all those trees,' she said, 'how I saw the many dreams I had composed for myself in the arrogance of youth. And I saw on those trees that . . .'

'I remember to forget,' Old Man said, 'how that strange tribe systematically eliminated me from their routines and finally drove me to the edge of their mountains. I must try to forget the starvation and the suffering and how I had to eat wood and roots for many days.'

'. . . the real failure of my life,' Old Woman said, 'was that I had dreamt at all and I had too many dreams and I chased them till I grew old in sorrow. For the dreams grew up too and deserted me. And when he had been driven from the city I knew that I could never dream any more. I was considered a success but I was dying inside and nobody knew it. And I saw on all those trees that our houses were burnt down and every single thing I had done had disappeared. Now I am here with nothing behind me and nothing before me except chaining Pinprop and listening to him for the rest of the days of my life.'

'I thought I was going to die but . . .'

'We have no time,' bellowed Pinprop, butting in, 'to stand here to remember and forget. This table is heavy on my head.'

'Chain the insolent clown!' screamed Old Woman.

'Cut him to pieces!' shouted Old Man.

'Castrate him!'

'He is already castrated.'

'Then do it again.'

'Let's chop off his fingers,' snarled Old Man.

'I'm starving.'

'Let us at least arrive first,' said Pinprop, emolliently.

'A sound idea,' agreed Old Man.

'I'm tired,' said Old Woman.

'Let's proceed.'

'A yes to all that,' said Pinprop.

Then they were gone into the depth of the silence, into which a faint music was receding.

Six

In the silence of the clearing the young man and young woman were still lying on the ground.

'It's very quiet here,' the young man said.

'I can hear a baby crying.'

'That's strange. I can't hear anything.'

'Can't you hear a baby crying?'

'No.'

'That's a shame.'

'Why?'

'It sounds like our baby.'

'Our baby? What a sweet sound it must be.'

'Actually, it isn't. It's an irritating sound.'

'I wish I could hear it,' said the young man.

'So do I.'

Seven

Silence settled on them like dew.

'It's very quiet all of a sudden,' the young woman said.

'Yes. It is.'

'I do wish someone would come along.'

'So do I.'

'I feel very lonely.'

'It's not a nice feeling, is it?'

'I wish we could find a room. Any room, where I can just lie in bed and stay there for the rest of my life.'

'I wish we could.'

'Stop mimicking me,' said the young woman.

'I didn't mean to.'

'Shall we go and look for a room?'

'I don't think we will find one. But trying might give us something to do.'

'The only reason I might get up from here,' said the young woman, 'is if I know that at some point we might find a place where we can just be.'

'A place to learn how to dream again.'

'A place to learn how to forget.'

'A place to be compassionate.'

'Any old dump would do.'

'It has to be a special place, though,' said the young man.

'Any rundown squat would do.'

'It has to be full of magic and love and lovely lights.'

'Any old dustbin is fine for me.'

'I'll settle for the sky.'

'I'll settle for a piece of bread.'

'Yes. I'm hungry.'

'I could eat you if we had a fire.'

'I wouldn't like to eat you. I might make a delicacy out of kissing you, though.'

'If we don't stop talking,' said the young woman, 'we will never find us a place.'

'Let's talk a bit more. We never get a chance to talk.'

'Are you feeling better?'

'No. Are you?'

'Not really.'

'My throat feels as if it's made of gleet.'

'That's gut-rot.'

'It feels like I've got a lump of lead in there and I can't swallow it down.'

'That sounds bad.'

'How is your throat?'

'Bad. But I don't feel like celebrating my illness right now.'

'That's a good idea.'

'Shall we get going?'

'Why not? I don't know if I can manage it, though.'

'I don't know if I can either.'

'Let's try anyway.'

'Yes.'

'I'm ready when you are,' said the young man.

Eight

After a short silence, a heavier silence, the young woman said:

    'Let's have an argument.'

    'I'm too tired.'

    'Come on.'

    'Okay.'

    'What should we argue about?'

    'I don't know.'

    'Why not?'

    'Because I don't.'

    'What do you mean you don't?'

    'I don't.'

    'You are an idiot, that's why.'

    'No, I'm not.'

Nine

The silence became gentler.

'Let's go, then,' said the young woman.

'Yes. Let's go.'

'Let's go holding hands.'

'Dreaming about wonders.'

'That sounds nice.'

'Let's go in such closeness that the world will be astonished that, amidst such devastation, beauty and truth can still exist and two souls can still participate in the imagination of life.'

'Let's do that,' said the young woman, 'while you help me up.'

'Let's go in such unity . . .'

Raising her voice, the young woman said:

'Do you want to help me up or not?'

'Sorry.'

'Come on, then.'

Ten

The young man got up from the ground, clearly in some pain, and then helped her up. After they were standing, they still kept the distance between them.

'I hope we find the room,' the young woman said.

'Yes. I feel tired.'

'Let's go, then.'

'In unity and love.'

'Let's just go.'

'In peace and tranquillity.'

'Forget the clichés. Just come on.'

'Alright . . .'

'What's the matter now?'

'I'm trying,' said the young man, 'to catch a thought.'

'Well go on, then. But be quick about it.'

'It's a lovely thought.'

'Get on with it and let's go.'

'I need the right atmosphere. I need silence.'

Eleven

The silence he needed wasn't there.

    'If I don't say the thought right,' said the young man, 'I might destroy it.'

Twelve

The young man waited, patiently. Then he spoke.

'Life is a masterpiece of the imagination,' he said.

'Is that it?'

'Yes. Don't you think it is lovely?'

'The imagination of a sick mind, I would say. Let's go.'

'It's a shame you don't like it. That is the best thought I've had in my whole life.'

'Let's go.'

'The best thought of my life and it's gone in a twinkle.'

'I'm sure you'll survive the disappointment.'

'My darling, let's go.'

'Yes. Let's.'

'Let's go slowly.'

'And with dignity.'

'Holding the best moments of our lives like a bottle of wine.'

'Like a glass of water.'

'Water, yes, water. I could do with some water.'

'I'm thirsty.'

'I'm parched.'

'Let's go.'

'Dreaming about water.'

There was silence. Then they left the clearing in opposite directions.

Book Four

One

In another clearing in the forest there stood a white building with a blue door. On the door was the legend: 'Eden. Closed for restoration.'

Old Man and Old Woman sat impassively in a far corner of the clearing. Pinprop emerged from the forest with the table on his head, which he deposited in front of the old couple.

'I'm definitely exhausted,' he said.

He sat on the ground.

'A new arrival, I hope.'

He laughed.

'I wish you both weren't being so quiet.'

There was silence.

'It's been a long journey, I suppose. I don't even feel like being talkative now that you are both so quiet.'

He laughed again.

'A yes to this, a no to that. Yes, sir, yes, madam. A solid yes. The vote is taken. Skeletons. Biographical trees. Routines and routines. Tiredness, sir, and old age. Slavery and acceptance. Secret freedom. A dance to all that, sir and madam. A dance and a song.'

He giggled.

'I've carried both of you for so long that I feel like a hunchback. And now you are both silent. Definitely a dance and a song.'

Pinprop got up, shook his feet, and walked crab-like around Old Man and Old Woman. He performed an absurd little dance. He laughed again. Then he sat back on the ground, in front of them, cross-legged.

Two

'I'm tired,' said Old Man, waking up.

'I'm tired,' said Old Woman.

'Pinprop, have we arrived?'

'Oh, sir, em, only temporarily.'

'Why aren't you being long-winded?' asked Old Woman.

'I feel as if I've taken on both your ages.'

'I wish we could hang him,' she said.

'Yes. Hang him by his testicles.'

'That's a good idea.'

'Let's arrive first,' Old Man suggested.

'I'm tired.'

'Let's sleep.'

'I'm afraid of sleeping.'

'Let's not talk about fear.'

'Fear, fear, fear,' said Pinprop.

'Stop it,' cried Old Man.

'Terror, terror, terror.'

'Shut up,' cried Old Woman.

'They are just words,' said Pinprop.

'Words can be made manifest,' said Old Woman.

'Too many of them have been,' said Old
Man.

'Pinprop, where are we?'

'Somewhere, madam.'

'A most satisfactory answer.'

'Definitely pointed,' agreed Old Man.

Three

After a short silence Pinprop laughed.

'Slave,' Old Man said, 'why are you laughing?'

'Can I be dishonest?'

'Certainly. That breeds proper under-standing,' said Old Woman.

'A stupid question, Pinprop. You know how much we . . .'

'Well, sir and madam. The thought struck me . . .'

'Where?' enquired Old Woman.

'And how did it strike you?' enquired Old Man.

'In a flash,' said Pinprop.

'I never saw it,' said Old Woman.

'Well, the thought struck me . . .'

'Again!' said Old Man. 'What a solid head you must have.'

'Stony, I would think,' Old Woman said.

'Anyway the thought occurred to me . . .'

'The thought has suddenly changed its form,' said Old Man.

'A new chemistry, no doubt,' observed Old Woman.

'Will you listen to me, both of you,' Pinprop said loudly, almost shouting.

Four

There was a long silence. Then:

'Hysterical insolence!' cried Old Woman.

'Unforgivable rebellion!' cried Old Man.

'I suggest a chaining, a skinning and a hanging.'

'All at once.'

'With great celebration.'

'And relief.'

'Let's proceed at once,' cried Old Woman.

'Definitely.'

'I'm tired.'

'I'm tired.'

'I can't move.'

'I can't move.'

'Let's sleep on it.'

'I can't sleep.'

'I can't sleep either,' said Old Woman.

Five

'The thought occurred to me,' said Pinprop, after a short silence, 'that both of you are beginning to look like skeletons.'

'Blasphemy!' roared Old Man.

'Utter humiliation!' screeched Old Woman.

'Pinprop, you shall suffer for this a thousand thousand times.'

'You shall suffer in all the pits with all the world's vermin as your companions.'

'Then I shall never starve,' said Pinprop.

'You shall weep for eternity and no one will hear your weeping.'

'Your thoughts will strangle you and you shall never find death,' said Old Woman.

'Nor ever arrive anywhere.'

'Nor ever have a wash.'

'Nor ever . . .'

'Nor ever . . .'

'Let's sleep on it,' Old Man said.

'Let's try to sleep.'

'You shall be a slave for the rest of your life.'

'Let us sleep.'

'I'm tired or I would have heaped all the abuses in this world on him.'

'My mouth is heavy.'

'We still love you, Pinprop.'

'We always will,' said Old Woman.

'That is why you shall forever be our slave.'

'Even in sleep.'

'Yes. Sleep,' Old Man said.

Six

They fell silent. Then, in the distance, there was the sound of the siren again.

'Horrors!' cried Pinprop.

Then, in the woods and in the air, there was the sudden sound of birdsong, and a baby crying.

'Defilement!' said Pinprop.

Not long afterwards the young man and young woman stumbled into the clearing. They were chained together at the ankles.

Seven

'Let's rest here for a while,' said the young man.

    'Yes, let's do that.'

    Then they sat down on the ground, as far from one another as possible.

    'Let's sleep,' said the young man.

    'And forget.'

    'And remember.'

    'With no confusions.'

    'Or regrets.'

    'With no need to conform.'

    'Or be anything.'

    'With a lot of space to create,' said the young woman.

    'Without pain.'

    'Except my heart.'

    'And my throat.'

    'Tiredness.'

    'In perfect peace.'

    'And a few arguments now and then.'

    'Without wonder or beauty.'

    'Without anything.'

    'Except our past.'

'And each other.'
'With a few routines.'
'And we shall call it love.'
'Then we shall invent a new religion.'
'I'm lonely.'
'Let's sleep,' said the young man.

Eight

The siren sounded in the forest. Then, after the sound faded, the Man wandered into the clearing, dejected, dragging his feet.

'Water. Just water,' he said. 'I think I stink like old cheese.'

He fell silent.

'I should have stayed at the asylum. It's not my fault that I killed that sniffer.'

He laughed.

'It must be sad to be a sniffer. Sniff, sniff, sniff.'

He paused.

'I wish I had some water. Just a glass. I could wash with a few drops, drink a few more drops, and save the rest for later.'

He looked around and, for the first time, saw the white building with the blue door.

'Ah,' he said.

He read out the legend on the door.

'Room to Let.'

He was silent.

'Liars. Cheats. Thieves. Deceivers,' he cried out, suddenly. 'This is not a house. This isn't what I've been looking for. There's no room in there. It's a bloody prison, a bird cage, a trap. Sniff, sniff. I'm not going in there.'

There was another silence.

'I'm tired of running, running,' he said, dejectedly. 'Search, searching. Sniff, sniffing.'

He paused again, as a new thought came to life in him.

'I'd be much better off looking for them. Better to start from where I know. Escape to what I am. Grow on my own cross.'

He looked at the white building again.

'It's a joke.'

He made a long crying sound.

'A bad joke.'

He laughed. Then the silence was broken by the siren in the forest. The sounds came closer.

'They are nearby,' he said. 'Oh, good. Start again from where I know. Find what I am. Redeem myself. The asylum is as good a place as any. Who knows, maybe this whole planet is an asylum, a penal realm. A place for hard cases.'

The siren intensified.

'I must find them,' said the Man.

The siren sounded now with greater clarity.

'Lovely water,' he shouted loudly, suddenly. 'Where are you? Where are you?'

Then, as if in surrender to a new freedom, a new destiny, he ran out from the clearing into the forest, in the direction of the pure beauty of the sound of the siren.

'Water. Good water!' he cried, in the depths of the echoing woods.

'Waaaatttteeeerrrrr!!'

And then there was silence.

Nine

Out of the stillness, the young man spoke.
    'Are you alright?'
    'No.'
    'Let's go, then.'
    'I'm hurting all over.'
    'That's very good.'
    'How about you?'
    'I'm in agony.'
    'That's wonderful.'
    'Shall we go, then?'
    'With all this pain?'
    'Yes.'
    'That's a good idea.'
    'Yes.'
    'Where are we going?'
    'Let's just go.'
    'Yes.'
    'Can you help me up?'
    'Alright.'

Ten

The young woman helped the young man up and they went in the direction of the white building with the blue door, and saw it for the first time. They stopped in front of it.

'What a lovely anthill,' said the young woman.

'It's more like a junk-heap.'

'Without doubt an anthill.'

'Most certainly a junk-heap.'

'Nonsense.'

'Like most junk-heaps.'

'Absolute rubbish.'

'You're getting closer.'

'I hate you,' said the young woman.

'I hate you too,' said the young man.

'Let's go.'

Then, with clumsy feet, they left the clearing. As they entered the forest the young man tripped, but recovered his balance. Chained together, they disappeared into the forest, but left their silence behind.

Eleven

When they had gone their silence lingered.
Then Pinprop spoke.

'Now for some peace,' he said.

He giggled. He got up from his cross-
legged position in front of the table. He sang
a song to himself, and he danced.

'Definitely an arrival,' he said.

He went over to the white building with
the blue door.

'Most definitely the room,' he added.

He laughed.

'And so again and again, in an epic
journey, in exile, after falling and rising,
toiling and becoming hunchbacked, I find
only silence. How crude,' he said.

He danced a step.

'The trap becomes a mouse,' he said,
quoting himself. 'Most certainly. Beaten,
crushed underfoot, prey to a thousand
seasons of sickness. Tedium, neurosis, bore-
dom. Beaten and beaten till you laugh and
sing and say Yes! Yes! to everything.'

Pinprop danced another step.

'A most wonderful concept-room,' he said. 'Hah. I remember. All that iron. Stupidity, rubbish, routines, violence and then the illusion of happiness. Impotence. Just that and little else. Except lies. That's fun, though. I used to know an idiot. "Our lives are composed of too many lies," he would say. And that was a lie in itself.'

He fell silent.

'Now for some peace,' he said.

He was silent again.

'A room at last. An end to all our wandering.'

Twelve

Then, in the silence, a New Woman and a New Man, both apparently naked, emerged from the blue door of the white building. They sighed as one and stretched as one. Then, very slowly, they went to the far corners of the clearing. One went to the left, the other to the right. They stared serenely at the world before them.

Thirteen

'Or maybe it's a prison,' Pinprop said. 'It doesn't matter anyway. Anything can be put to good use. Anything can be reinvented. A solid yes to all that.'

Pinprop danced a step. Then he laughed. Then he turned grim.

Fourteen

Old Man and Old Woman sat in the white building. Pinprop sat at their feet. Everywhere else was in darkness, except Pinprop. He sat in light.

'I wish both of you could see this place,' said Pinprop. 'It's a wonderful room. Eight feet by ten. Large enough for the whole world.'

He was silent.

'There's nothing in it at all,' he continued. 'But there is an interesting smell in here. A very interesting smell indeed.'

He was silent.

'Is there anything either of you would like me to do?' he asked.

Silence.

'I don't suppose so.'

Pinprop laughed. He sang a song. Then, shouting into the silence, he said:

'Slave, slave, let there be light.'

Silence.

'Let there be light, slave,' he shouted again.

The light that was on Pinprop turned instantly to darkness.

'Ah,' he said. 'The word made manifest. Now for some peace.'

There was a long silence.

'It's a shame they are going to break it down soon.'

More silence.

'It's definitely a shame.'

He gave a short laugh. Then there was silence.

Beyond

One

New Man and New Woman spoke in the darkness. They spoke like children discovering light. Much time had passed and no time at all.

'Now let's start again,' said New Man.
'And again.'
'Go back to the earth.'
'To simple beginnings.'
'To what nourishes.'
'To what grows.'
'To sunlight.'
'And flowing water.'
'To inner light.'
'And fresh air.'
'Good breathing.'
'And sweet silence.'
'To new dancing.'
'And music.'

Two

'Let's go back to the source,' said New Woman.
    'Of rivers.'
    'Of worlds.'
    'Of dreams.'
    'Of realities.'
    'Of friendship.'
    'Of fellowship.'
    'Of what the heart feels.'

Three

'Let's dream again,' said New Man.
'Like we used to as kids.'
'Of Eden when it was new.'
'And after we have restored it.'
'With love.'
'And courage.'
'With patience.'
'And wisdom.'

Four

'Let's play again,' said New Woman.
        'As on the first day.'
        'When we were the garden.'
        'And the garden was us.'

Five

'Let's be happy again,' said New Man.

'As on the first day.'

'When all love was ours.'

'As it still is.'

'And always will be,' they both said together, as one.

A Note on the Form

The following tales are properly 'stokus'. A stoku is an amalgam of short story and *haiku*. It is story as it inclines towards a flash of a moment, insight, vision or paradox.

Its origin is mysterious, its purpose is revelation, its form compact, its subject infinite. Its nature is enigma as it finds tentative form in fiction, like the figure materialising from a cloud, or a being emerging from a vaporous block of marble.

By means of the stoku, that which was unknown reveals, in the medium of words, a translated existence. Thus worlds unknown can come into being in a lightning flash from the darkness of the mind.

Stokus are serendipities, caught in the air, reverse lightning.

I offer them humbly as tales found on the shore, in enchanted dawns.

Belonging

I had gone into a house by accident or maybe not. Originally I was searching for Margaret House, a mansion block. Anyway I went into this flat and the man of the house took me for his in-law, whom he had never met, or had met once before, a long time ago. He began saying things to me confidentially, telling me how he disapproved of some acquaintance, and how we should do this that or other, and how my wife did or didn't do what she was supposed to do, and he bared his heart and said many intimate things.

I watched him. When the misunderstanding began I tried to correct his error, but he seemed so keen to believe who I was and he was so absent-minded and yet single-minded in his rattling on that I didn't get a moment to correct his mistaking me for someone else.

Besides, I found I rather began to enjoy it. I enjoyed being someone else. It was fascinating. It was quite a delight suddenly finding myself part of a ready-made family, finding myself belonging. The thrill of belonging was wonderful.

The flat was cluttered with items of a rich family life. It was obviously a large extended family. The man who was addressing me was making food for a feast, adding ingredients for a cake, mixing condiments for a sauce, and it all smelt good. The enveloping party and family mood quite intoxicated me.

I began to think that maybe I was the man he took me for. And that if he saw me as another then maybe I *was* that other. Maybe I'd just woken from a dream into a reality in which I was who he thought I was, and that my old identity belonged to the dream. But as I toyed with this notion there was a growing sense in me that any minute the real person that was expected would turn up. Or, if not, that the wife of the real person would turn up, and would not recognise me.

The fear increased in me. Any minute now I would be unmasked. What would I do then? I felt awful. I dreaded it. I hadn't got myself into this deliberately. I hadn't even spoken a word during the whole time I was in that room, being mistaken for someone else. I wanted to belong. I wanted to belong there.

A sentence of unmasking, like death, hung over me. I waited, and listened to the man of the house talking, as time ticked away, bringing closer my inevitable disgrace.

Before I had strayed into that flat I had been going to meet a relation, my last living relation. It was, it seemed, the last stop for me in the world. I had nowhere else to go. Now I had this family, with food and a festival atmosphere promised. And yet . . .

And then, as I stood there, the door behind me opened. A black, Arabic, pock-marked, elderly gentleman came into the room, and I knew instantly that this was the man I had been mistaken for. He had the quiet and unmistakable authority of being who he was, the real in-law. And my first shock was that I looked nothing like him at all. I was younger, fresher, better-looking. I had vigour and freedom. I wasn't trapped by tradition. I was lithe. I could go any which way. I had many futures open to me. This man seemed seemed weighed down. There was an air about him of one whose roads were closed, whose future was determined, whose roles were fixed. He was, in the worst sense of the word, middle-aged; with no freedom, even to think independent thoughts. All this I sensed in a flash, but realised fully only afterwards. But I was profoundly shocked to have been mistaken for this man.

At the very moment the in-law entered the flat, the man of the house, who'd mistaken me in the first place, looked up, saw the real in-law, and knew him to be the one. I think he recognised him. How unobservant can people be! Anyway, at that instant he turned to me and, in outrage, said:

'And who are you?'

I think events swam before my eyes after that. My unmasking was very public. Suddenly people appeared from thin air, and were told in loud voices about my impersonation of the in-law. There were vigorous comments and curses and stares of amazement. People glared at me as though I were a monstrous criminal. Women regarded me darkly from behind veils. I feared for my life. Soon I was out in the street, surrounded by a crowd, by the community of an extended family. I was holding out a map and was saying:

'It was a mistake. I was looking for Margaret House, or Margaret Court.'

During the whole commotion I saw the name of the place I'd been looking for on the next building. I bore their outrage and their loud comments silently. Then after a while I set off for the building next door, my original destination. But the man of the house, who'd mistaken me for the in-law, said:

'Don't go there. You don't want to go there.'

Then I looked towards Margaret House. I looked at the grounds. I saw people milling about, in aimless circles. They twitched, moved listlessly, or erratically. They were dark forms, in dark overcoats, and their bodies were all shadows, as if they were in Hades. They moved as if they had invisible lead weights on their feet. They seemed to have no sense of anything. The courtyard was of concrete, but their collective presence made it look dark and sinister and touched with unpredictable danger. There was the merest hint that they were mad . . .

I started to go in that direction, but, after the man of the house spoke, I stopped. I could feel the disturbed wind from the people milling about in an evil shade, in the courtyard of Margaret House. Then I changed direction, and went back towards the crowd, then out to the street, towards a life of my own.

The Mysterious Anxiety of Them and Us

We were in the magnificent grounds of our mysterious host. A feast had been laid out in the open air. There were many of us present. Some were already seated and some were standing behind those seated. In a way there were too many of us for the food served, or it felt like that.

There was a moment when it seemed that everyone would rush at the food and we'd have to be barbaric and eat with our hands, fighting over the feast laid out on the lovely tables. The moment of tension lasted a long time.

Our host did nothing, and said nothing. No one was sure what to do. Insurrection brooded in the wind. Then something strange happened. Those who were at table served themselves, and began eating. We ate calmly. My wife was sitting next to me. The food was wonderful.

We ate with some awareness of those behind us, who were not eating, and who did not move. They merely watched us eating.

Did we who were eating feel guilty? It was a complex feeling. There is no way of resolving it as such. Those who were at table, ate. That's it. That's all.

We ate a while. Then the people behind us began to murmur. One of them, in a low voice, said:

'The first person who offers us some food will receive . . .'

I was tempted to offer them some food. But how could I? Where would I start? The situation was impossible. If you turned around, you would see them all. Then your situation would be polarised. It would be you and them. But it was never that way to begin with. We were all at the feast. It's just that you were at the table, and you began to eat. They weren't at table, and they didn't eat. They did nothing. They didn't even come over, take a plate, and serve themselves. No one told them to just stand there watching us eat. They did it to themselves.

So to turn around and offer them food would automatically be to see them, and treat them as inferior. When in fact they behaved in a manner that made things turn out that way.

And so we continued to eat, and ignored the murmurs. Soon we had finished eating. We were satisfied, and took up the invitation to explore other parts of the estate. There was still plenty of food left, as it happened.

My wife and I were almost the last to leave the table. As we got up, I looked behind us. I was surprised to see only three people there. Was that all? They had seemed like more, like a crowd. Maybe there had been more of them, but they'd drifted off, given up, or died.

While we had been eating it had often occurred to me that there was nothing to stop them from sticking knives into our backs.

My wife and I filed out with the others, towards the gardens, in the sumptuous grounds of that magnificent estate.

It had been a dreamy day of rich sunlight.

The Clock

It took place in the Bois du Boulogne, on a sombre moonlit night. We stood in a clearing among the chestnut trees. We were all in eighteenth-century costume.

The moment arrived. The duellists stood opposite one another, with their pistols primed. Then the most unlikely thing happened. The man whose second I was, whom I partly knew, suddenly cried out. He pointed at something in the midriff of his enemy. We looked to see what troubled him. We saw a large, round, shining clock about his enemy's waist. He wore it like the buckle of a belt. The numbers were black against the luminous dial.

My acquaintance was mesmerised by the clock. He was transfixed by it. He kept pointing. Then he began gibbering. The clock had somehow poisoned his mind. I said:

'For God's sake, old chap. It's only a clock.'

'Look at it!' he whispered. 'It's fiendish!'

'Take your mind off it,' I said.

'That's impossible! It's an abomination!'

His enemy stood impassively with his second. They gazed at us. My acquaintance fell apart before my eyes. He was utterly unable to rid his mind of the clock. I hadn't wanted the damn duel anyway. I had no idea what its cause had been, and was never told. It remained a secret between the two enemies. I had got roped into it by honour, false friendship, and favours I owed. Damn the favours one owes. They lead one into other people's hell.

There was nothing anyone could do. My acquaintance had succumbed to an appalling paralysis. His enemy had been patient. Night darkened, and then dawn slowly appeared. His enemy had waited many hours for my acquaintance to recover. He waited silently, like a monument, a stone statue of some disdainful Roman god.

My acquaintance, however, became less than human with the agonising passing of time. Shivering, muttering about the infernal nature of the clock, my acquaintance had a mental breakdown as dawn broke. Eventually we had to carry him from the middle of the clearing to the waiting coach. It had been understood that there would be only one coach, the loser being presumed to have been killed.

We had to take the coach. The enemy was magnanimous. He was silent. He was as implacable as a marble figure on a plinth at night in a strange city. He and his allies simply stood there in the gathering dawn, with the luminous clock brilliant about his solar plexus.

My acquaintance never recovered. We took him to a hospital. Then his halluci-nations began. Then his madness.

I visited him often. Whenever he saw me he asked about the clock. I was evasive in my answers. Then I stopped going to see him. He was infecting me with his instability. It doesn't take much, does it, to unhinge a man. Especially if, in a clearing, at night, under a moonlit sky, a mind can't unfix itself from a symbol.

Now I go through life not fixing my mind on anything, or anyone. There is a sort of freedom in this.

Music for a Ruined City

1

I have been wandering around in a bombed-out city. I have seen devastated streets, broken bridges, flattened houses. The glass fronts of shops were all smashed, their goods looted. The commercial district was a mass of rubble. I saw piano shops with mangled instruments. Everything was in chaos.

I saw unforgettable things. I saw a community stoned to death in their sleep. This happened on the top of a multi-storeyed building. They were asleep in their white tents and people of a different sect came with rocks and stoned them to death while they dreamt.

2

Then there was that lovely building where a crowd of mourners were gathered outside. An Arabic bishop was on the floor, weeping. When he got up he held out a piece of yellow-coloured glass, and pointed. On the floor about him were blue and green and yellow fragments. Then all became clear. It was a Christian church. The whole church front had been made sublime with stained glass depicting images of the saints and cameos from the New Testament. The church was in ruins, the stained glass shattered. It was only when I was shown a picture of how beautiful it used to be that I realised the magnitude of the damage.

3

It was a city under occupation. The white presence was resented by the people. Nothing worked. I had gone to a makeshift government office with an insider. Two white men were in front of me. We were all supposed to be searched and had to leave our passports and be given tokens. The two white men went through and weren't searched and didn't have to leave their passports. When I went past, however, the officials pounced on me. Somewhat irritated, I threw my passport on the table. To the smirking official, I said:

'You complain about being in a state of occupation and yet you waive your rules for your occupiers. But you treat me like I'm a criminal. One rule for those who bomb you, another rule for the rest. Hypocrites!'

I took my token and left. I was annoyed, but my annoyance freed me from illusion.

4

And yet I could not detach myself from the destruction wrought on this ancient city. Its famous museum had been plundered of its timeless artefacts, its libraries robbed of priceless books and manuscripts. Districts were terrorised by newly unleashed gangs. There was an uprising of religious sects. Homes were raided. People were set upon, and massacred. A culture was in free fall, in meltdown, descending into inferno. There was anarchy and hopelessness everywhere. And yet I glimpsed a certain resilience in the people, a stoical fatalism.

5

These are journeys in the hyper-realism of a suffering city. Wherever I go, I see veiled mothers in black, wailing. They cry out the stories of their dead children, or their missing husbands.

6

But somewhere in this tragic city an orchestra strikes up. A performance of music begins. Strains of a classical air seep out from the fabulous concert hall, one of the few buildings untouched by the seven-day bombardment. No one knows who the people are within. They listen to music that enchants and cleanses the spaces of suffering. There time stands suspended, and a pure joy percolates out from the orchestra, out and up, in a spiral, to the sky and the stars. This is a music alien to all around it, to the bombed-out city, but casting a spell, changing what it touches. Such beauty can be a denial and an affront to all this tragedy.

But to hear Mozart in a bombed city: how much more beautiful it sounds, as if it were composed to somehow soothe the ruins, to promise a wiser future rising from the rubble.

7

I go on wandering among the broken columns, witnessing the faces of mute grief, with Mozart in my heart, like ice over a wound.

The Unseen
Kingdom

1

There is a fair, which takes place in the south of France, where books are treated like roses. Writers are rarely invited to attend.

Books are displayed on long tables, with their pages open, and with crushed flowers on their open pages. The books scent the air with gentle dreams. There is indeed a mysterious mood about the place, a dawn-coloured enchantment, on account of the open books.

The lady who runs the fair wears a silk scarf and is a lady of great devotion and tenderness. She is much loved in the community of booksellers and publishers. She goes about unobtrusively, wandering among the stalls as between paths in a delightful garden of many-coloured flowers. She is responsible for the books, the attendances, the display of rare illuminated manuscripts, and she does it all with exquisite taste.

The main focus of interest this season are the Lewis Carroll books. There are many items being shown for the first time. It is a

charming collection of manuscripts, photo-
graphs and pages of correspondence. One of
his family's descendants is attending, to lend
an extra quaintness to the festival.

This year, also, an immaculate fraud has
been perpetrated. A delicate scandal scents
this rarefied air of books. No one talks about it
openly. It is there, floating about in the
charmed mood, and only the lady who
organises the fair appears not to know about
this delicious scandal. It seems that a writer
has been rigged into winning the prestigious
festival prize with forged nomination letters.
It seems this forgery has put everyone under
suspicion. A secret investigation is launched.
All the publishers co-operate.

It is a lovely fair, and my first time
attending. The lounge is beautiful, the
restaurant restful, and browsing through the
exhibition of books proved to be one of the
most magical experiences I've had.

I gazed into books that took me away to
distant kingdoms where I was instantly
happy. In the world of these special books
there is no stress, only a kind of peace, and
a freedom, and a sense of having been
redeemed into a weightless condition of pure

beauty. The imagination renews the world like dawn does.

And yet this whispering scandal grows. Someone here, amidst all these flowers, has ruined the innocence of our faces. In this labyrinth of beauty, under a clear sky, there is someone whose face is not what it seems.

I linger among the pages of distant realms. Books from all over the universe are here. The tethered balloons are all outside. Most of us have come here in usual modes of transportation, but this year balloons borne aloft are the most favoured way.

2

Towards the evening a bald man with a rock-like head was seen walking through the fair. He was a hired hand for hard jobs. He was next seen sitting on a wooden chair, giving an account, cap in hand, to the one who had commissioned him. He had done satis-factorily what he had been told to do, making everyone a suspect. It was now impossible to separate the innocent from the guilty.

When he had finished giving his report, the hired hand disappeared into the unsuspecting crowd. The rigged condition lingered, but it meant nothing, it changed nothing. For here, in this fair, the only thing that matters is the charmed condition of books that endure. It is impossible, in the long run, to rig a book into a magic condition, or make it give off a light it does not have.

3

And so the lady of the fair wandered among the flowering books untouched by the scandal. And the scandal itself was soon dissolved by the higher truth and the beautiful light that protects this place from all evil.

The air is clear again. The books breathe out a timeless peace and an eternal youth into the festival. It is as though nothing untoward had happened here, or ever could.

The Racial Colourist

This happened during the war. A group of us were sitting on a wall, and I was trying to get these two people to meet. But one of them was a racial colourist. He had a chart in one hand and paste on his fingertips. He told me there was no way he could shake hands with a third-rate white man. I was surprised, because this chap too was white, and he would receive a hug from me but he wouldn't touch another white man whom he considered inferior. The other man was so offended that he stormed off. I went after him, but he walked away so fast he disappeared. As I went back to the group, I became aware for the first time of the danger of my position.

The man who began it all had gone. I stood among the rest, ill at ease. I had no way of telling who was a racial colourist. Then I noticed a white youth in the place of the man who had gone. He wore little round glasses. He kept looking at me in a peculiar way. I tried to ignore him. A girl went past and waved at me. She was someone I knew. The youth with the glasses consulted his colour chart and then made an urgent call with a walkie-talkie.

'Yes, sir. He said hello to one of ours. Yes, yes, sir.'

It was clear he was monitoring the contact I had with people of accepted racial purity. I became aware that he belonged to a shadowy organisation. What else do they do? Do they murder people like me? I felt unsafe. I hurried away from the group. The bespectacled youth, with his chart, and his walkie-talkie, came after me. I crossed a field, at a near run. He picked up speed. Where was I running to, where could I run to, where was safe for me? It grew dark. The chap kept on my trail, pursuing me. I lost him across a whispering maze of fields. Soon it was night. Then suddenly I saw him in the distance, with a torch in his hand. He walked alongside the nocturnal silence of a village green. Behind him, revealed in a blue flash of lightning, was a quaint provincial town. A voice within me said:

'Go towards him. Don't run away. Go menacingly, purposefully. He's more scared of you than you are of him.'

So I stopped running. And as I strode towards him, with a mean purpose in me, he appeared to hesitate. When I neared him I gazed into his eyes. Behind his glasses, he had scared, timid eyes and an ordinary harmless face which I didn't have the heart to hurt in any way. I brushed past him in the dark. I went towards the village. I didn't look back. I didn't care any more.

The Black Russian

The first time we failed but, this time, we will succeed in filming our version of *Eugene Onegin*, in splendid technicolour.

There were four of us. We were going to use the local tools available. One of us had to be in the kitchen, in charge of the taper. When the train approached the one in the kitchen had to light the taper. This was a sign to the train driver to keep the train's fire blazing, and to maintain his speed. His fire and speed would then activate another scene, where one of the women on a bicycle would ride forth. And then somewhere else another character would do what he was supposed to do.

It was all so well co-ordinated, and depended utterly on a one-take success, a once-only event. It was then or never.

The taper caught fire, the train driver saw it, the other dependent scenes went off perfectly, and as the train sped past I jumped on the open-backed platform where, to my surprise, I encountered a black man who was an important worker on the luxury train. He was in charge of looking after the higher-ranking travellers. He was dressed beautifully in a red jacket with gleaming epaulettes. He had dark, almost blue skin. When I jumped on the platform of the moving train he smiled at me. Then, to my astonishment, he said:

'Welcome, Dubchanka,' as if he had known me all my life. He smiled again knowingly.

Whereupon I helped myself to one of his freshly cut and lovingly buttered sandwiches, with delicious slices of cheese. The one I chose had been bitten into by him, but I didn't mind. Then I jumped off the slowing train. The black Russian jumped down too. He ran elegantly towards the local shops to buy some caviar for the remaining sandwich, and to get other items for himself during the train's brief stop in town.

But someone else in our crew had jumped on the train's platform and, imitating me, had helped himself to the last of the splendid cheese sandwiches. I could see the black Russian's polite dismay as he watched the crew member devour his sandwich. It was so funny.

Anyway, all the scenes went off well. The school teacher had her moment. Kuragin had his. The train was beautiful and was painted black. Colours were so perfect on that day. The women played their roles excellently. All the co-ordinated filming had been a great success, and we knew in our hearts that we had brought home a great Russian classic. It was the last day of filming. We had done Pushkin proud, at last.

Wild Bulls

It is the aftermath of war, and there is chaos everywhere. I am in a fabulous house where they have gathered the children of war. They are all orphans and all lost. I am meant to be their teacher.

They can't absorb anything just yet, so I try to get them interested in art. To my surprise, they take to it. They paint and draw freely, for long hours, absorbed and lost in colour, fleeing from grief into a world of mysterious shapes, of bulls, birds, hybrid creatures, and patterns in which are concealed indeterminate beings.

I also try to get them to do other subjects, like maths, history, geography, but about these they are desultory. For them art is the thing.

After some time folks come visiting, acquaintances from various universities. They take an interest in what the children of war had been doing. They find little to remark upon in the general subjects. Then I show their art. The visitors are bowled over, thunderstruck. They are astounded at the paintings, in rich ochre, in reds and yellows, of enormous wild bulls. The canvases are large, and the paintings bristle with unaccountable energy and wildness.

There isn't one painting that isn't extraordinary, or terrifying, in some way. It is like beholding, on the walls of obscure caves, works of bold mature colourists, of the stature of the post-impressionists, or even the masters of expressionism. It is awesome, and spooky. Who on earth are these children? Has grief unhinged them into genius?

Later on we are at a large round table. It is the end of dinner. Most of us are writers. One of the writers, a woman, and celebrated, proposes that we each sing "thank you" in as many different languages as possible. I begin by doing so in the language of a favourite aria, with all the elaborated modulations required. The others sing in German, Japanese, Russian, Swahili . . .

There is good cheer among us. But it is a moment in an oasis, a brief respite from all the suffering around, in the aftermath of war.

Outside, children search for their mothers in bombed houses and cratered tower blocks.

At night, in the darkened city, children sleep on the rubble of their bombed-out homes, waiting for their parents to return from the dead.

The Legendary Sedgewick

1

A man called Sedgewick performed a legendary feat in our presence. He had been a great cricketer, but he wasn't a cricketer any more. He had gone beyond the game. For some time now he had been developing a new form.

There were many rumours about him. As he tended towards silence, the rumours hardened into facts. No-one knew where he lived, or what he did with his time. And so it was concluded by many that he did business with the devil. Others, more charitably, maintained that he occupied himself with a little harmless dabbling in alchemy.

He no longer played cricket in public, and hadn't done for years. In fact what he was perfecting was more like golfing cricket, for it was a strange amalgam he played.

And so we found ourselves oddly assembled for no particular reason, it seemed, except that those of us who hadn't seen him in years received a call asking us to witness an event as interesting as a brief meeting with a once-famous cricketer whose name recalled for us magical moments from our youth.

And there he was, unceremonious as ever. Not even a word or nod to acknowledge our presence. Just the merest hint of a smile, tender enough to charm us into a mood of expectancy that only nostalgia permits to those who have seen it all, and who no longer dream of new glories.

He stood in the woods and made a barely discernible spin-throw with the cricket ball. It travelled lightly from his hand, fell on the ground, rolled up the slope and span among the roots of a tree. Then, circling the tree, it went a short way on, and slipped into a brook.

We sighed in disappointment. But there was something about his smile, so we continued gazing at the ball in mild perplexity. Meanwhile the ball appeared to change consistency, appeared to float, but in truth it span back towards us, inching along the surface of the water. And, to the astonishment of the gathering crowd that sensed a legendary event was unfolding, the ball went on spinning backwards till it rolled out of the water, onto the land. Then, as if pushed by an invisible force, it made its way to the hole, and dropped in, to the tremendous applause of the crowd.

It was a miraculous throw, done with the greatest nonchalance, defying all known laws of motion and cricket. Instantly Sedgewick, a black chap, became a legend. He became internationally famous.

The next time we saw him he lived in a nice house. He attempted again a nonchalant throw, out of his frosted window. But he missed, twice. The third time, however, something began to happen. The ball, spinning, began its famous journey. And we watched, fascinated, to see what it would do, how it would get to that distant hole, from such a lackadaisical throw . . . .

2

Afterwards, we were all downstairs. There was Sedgewick, me, a few others, and a proper legend of the game – a man called Jackson. Now Jackson was *the* man. He was the most respected cricketer of them all. He was trim, he was alert, and Sedgewick had for him the highest regard.

We were all there, downstairs, outside, and the dapper Jackson was demonstrating a classical overarm bowl, with a wrist action that was his speciality. Sedgewick stood next to me, respectfully looking on at the moves of an acknowledged master. Sedgewick had an interesting air about him. His chemistry had changed. Jackson knew this. Jackson was a great player, but Sedgewick had done something truly magical and inexplicable. He had, it seemed, cracked the arcane art of the spin and speed rotation of the casual throw. He had mastered something so unique that no one even dreamt it was there to be mastered. His new ability, his mastery of a completely new and original skill, put him in an unfathomable class, a different space. And not even Jackson knew how to deal with it. Sedgewick's airy achievement made Jackson's legend seem ordinary, without allure, without mystery, without romance. Such was the mood that day.

Sedgewick, meanwhile, remained himself – simple, ordinary, plain. But the space he occupied was transformed by that strange knack of coolly flicking a ball with a twisting wrist movement. And the ball would travel, spin mysteriously, endlessly, up slopes, down, round, through obstacles, as if aided by an unseen power, right to the unexpected hole, in an art so fiendish that it amounted to sorcery . . . .

Perhaps rumours are a parallel kind of reality.

The Golden Inferno

The house was a country, and in front of it there was a gutter. And the gutter was clogged with things which made the air foul to breathe. There was a dead cow in it, with feet sticking out from the muddy water. This poisoned everything. There were thick books drowned in the gutter. It was suspected that there were dead human beings in there too, their arms also sticking out, barely discernible. A hospital bed rested, lopsided, on all this poisonous detritus. And on the bed were people who were ill because of the foulness of all that was concealed in the gutter and which was now leaking out to the whole world.

In the country that was a house I saw thousands of tables and pallets. On them were innumerable men and women stricken with a disease for which, as yet, there was no cure. They were an inferno of bodies, of dying people, in a nightmare from which there was no awakening except death. The rows of them seemed infinite.

On a stand, before a platform of dignitaries, the archbishop kept repeating the same words into a microphone:

'This is a husband and wife thing, a thing between husbands and wives.'

He didn't seem to know what else to say. He was trying to simplify the problem so that it could be dealt with, section by section.

Crowds of people were gathered. They had a tragic air.

The plague had plunged the world into gloom.

2

They eventually woke up to the dead cow and the drowned books and the dead bodies in the great gutter in front of the house that was a country. A world-famous popstar took an interest in the house and drew more attention to it. This made the house more conscious of itself. It took a lot of time for this to happen. Children played near the gutter and caught a mysterious illness and died. For a long time no-one did anything. All pretended the problem wasn't there. Or that it wasn't a problem.

On the tables and pallets women were naked and dying in the nightmare grip of the merciless disease. One woman was making sexual motions, writhing and making love to the air. This is not because it was what she wanted to do, but because the motion eased her agony.

There was a mist over all these bodies writhing like the condemned in a hell that no one has ever imagined. Millions of them were on the path to perishing. The world watched them die in their lonely mute agony.

Someone's thought circulated in the air, but was not expressed. Someone inwardly evil. The thought went: they should all be killed.

Who can harbour such a holocaustal notion, such a genocidal vision?

3

We had to watch them in their long lonely deaths. We tried to prevent more people from joining their numbers. So many thoughts circulated in the air. Some extreme, some spiritual, some practical, running in the underworld of our grief:

'We must change. Sex cannot be the angel of death of a whole people. If we master desire we will be transformed. We will become masters of ourselves, the magnet of a beautiful new future.'

4

It came about that one day the people in the house had simply had enough. A woman borrowed some boots and went into the gutter and began to probe and heave. Foul water ran into the boots, the stink was intolerable, but she was undeterred. She worked hard at clearing the mess. She worked alone. We watched and did not watch her. And then, gradually, people joined in. They waded into the great gutter. They lifted up the hospital bed and pulled out the sunken books. They hoisted out the dead cow and lowered it onto the back of a truck. They took it far away, and dug a very deep hole, and buried it. Some thought it should have been burnt. Others couldn't bear the thought of death in the air they breathed. They dug out corpses in the gutter and gave them decent burials too.

It was plenty for a day's work. A symbolic day. The gutter had other grim secrets, though. The hospital bed was still there, on the mud and detritus. But the gutter was less clogged than before. Fewer people were dying. Fewer people caught the mysterious disease. The people felt better about themselves. The long denial was over. Something was being done at last. Children could begin, tentatively, to play again in the house that was a country.

The Secret
Castle

The bus drove past telegraph poles in meadows of blue. In the bus, on that beautiful Italian day, there were boys returning from school, and working men. The bus came to a stop. A woman with several men came on. She was a young woman who carried herself gracefully. One of the boys helped her into the bus and gave up his window seat to her. She had an exquisite complexion, clear eyes, and uncanny composure. The boy, called Reggio, made friendly conversation with the young woman. The men she was with regarded Reggio with suspicion. He was just a boy, coming home from school, and he meant nothing by it. He was drawn by the mystery of the young woman, who sat impassively, staring straight ahead, as if she were dead, or going to die.

Her face, or, rather, her eyes lit up only when the boy spoke to her and asked questions, to which answers were not necessary. The questions were not necessary either, but life would be duller if he hadn't asked them.

'Do you like those hills?'

'Yes.'

'Do you like that cloud?'

'Yes.'

'Do you like that horse in the field?'

'Yes.'

'Do you like that car going past us?'

'No.'

'Do you like this bus?'

'Yes.'

'Do you like school?'

She paused. Her face clouded a little. Then she gave a tiny smile, like a snowdrop, and said:

'Yes.'

The boy was silent for a while. He was not thinking of any new questions, but just turning over in his mind the clarity of her answers. Somehow, darkly, he found he deduced a great deal from her slender answers, but he wasn't sure what. Decorum made him silent for longer, but the strangeness of her answers made him want to know more.

The young woman remained impassive, staring straight ahead, barely moving, barely breathing. He didn't look at her, but he seemed to see her. She gave him the peculiar feeling that she was like a calf being led off to the slaughter.

Then he noticed that she moved. It was a movement so odd, full of such contained intensity, that it seemed to demand him to speak some more.

'Do you like fields?'

'Yes.'

'Do you like rivers?'

'Yes.'

'Do you like roads?'

'No.'

He paused. He wasn't expecting that answer at all. He couldn't see anything wrong with roads. He quite liked roads. But now that he looked at roads through her spirit, he wasn't so sure. Maybe there was something unnatural about them after all. He wandered off in thought. Then, after a while, she made the same odd movement.

'Do you like houses?'

'Yes.'

'Do you like moonlight?'

'Yes.'

'Do you like mirrors?'

'No.'

This arrested him. For the first time he turned and gave her a quick look. He thought it strange that someone so beautiful should not like mirrors. He pondered this a long time. And time became elastic as he pondered. He lost himself in thought, and he lost himself in space. He was no longer in the bus, but in a magical world, a world that made him smile. He was within happiness itself, within its secret castle. When he came to, he found that the bus had stopped. It was the end of the journey. They all filed down. The men she was with regarded him darkly. When they had all got down on the dusty road, one of the men turned to him and asked what he meant by talking to the young woman.

'Nothing,' he said.

Then he apologised. The man grew angry at the apology: it seemed to confirm guilt. He got steamed up, he talked in a loud voice. He addressed the other men, and appealed to their common roots. The men crowded the boy. They were all shouting. Then a tall gangly man among them, a bit of a fool, set up his fists like a boxer in a comic movie. He began to jump around the boy. The men egged him on.

The boy was perplexed. He had no idea how things had come to this point. While the shadow-boxing went on around him, he caught a glimpse of the young woman. She was hidden behind the men. Confused, he felt a punch whistle past his face. Swiftly, he set up his fists too. Before he knew it he was grappled to the ground, his feet kicking the air. A heavy weight and smelly work clothes pressed down on him. Bad breath fanned his face. Bristles stabbed his cheek. There were voices all around, hollering.

Then, suddenly, he found himself standing up. His father, who was the bus driver, was beside him, shouting, waving his arms, defending his son.

'My son meant nothing by it. What does he know? Harmless questions. A polite young man. Gave up his seat. Meant nothing by it.'

'So you say,' one of the men cried. 'He's old enough to do enough damage. They start earlier and earlier these days.'

The voices flew back and forth. The boy stood there, a boy among men. The other school boys were a short way off, staring, whispering among themselves.

Then Reggio's father found a solution.

'I will solve this problem,' he said. 'I will solve it now.'

'How?' they asked.

'Get back on the bus. Everybody get back on the bus.'

After much discussion, in which nothing was really discussed, just voices flying out of mouths, they all trooped back on the bus. Then Reggio's father got into the driver's seat, started the vehicle, and they soon set off.

The young woman sat in the same place as she did before, near the window. Next to her was the man who shouted the loudest. He had a big jowled face, and severe eyes. He was squinting. He was a hard working man. Working his jaw. He looked like the word 'honour' in ragged clothes. He stared straight ahead. The young woman looked sideways out of the window. They did not speak. There was now a strange silence in the bus. Reggio was at the front, near his father.

The bus chugged across a bridge, past an orchard, an isolated villa, vineyards, a crumbling castle, and a field with a white horse staring at the sky. The bus drove past telegraph poles in meadows of blue.

Then the voices began again:

'Where is he taking us?'

'Yes, where is he going?'

They went on like that till they found themselves approaching a familiar place. The bus came to a halt. They were at the precise bus stop where the young woman and the men had first got on the bus. Reggio's father swung open the door.

'This is where you got on,' he said to the men. 'This is where you get off.'

There was a stunned silence. No-one moved. Then the young woman stood up. The man next to her was obliged to stand up too. She made her way down the aisle and when she got to the bus driver she stopped. Reggio did not look up at her. His father said:

'Everything should be simple.'

The young woman smiled; and when she smiled something beautiful shone from her, like the purity of that limpid sky. Then, with a barely perceptible movement, she passed something into the boy's hand.

'Yes,' she said, and gracefully got down from the bus.

The other men trooped after her morosely. They said nothing. They were working men, just trying to uphold their honour. The last to get down was the gangly fool who had wrestled young Reggio to the ground. He too was silent. But when the bus started to move he set up his fists again, as if challenging the departing bus to a fight.

Only then, as they departed, did Reggio look out of the window. Then, to his father, he said:

'But I meant nothing by it, Papa. Only harmless questions.'

'I know, my son,' the driver said. 'But they are the ones that can cause trouble.'

Reggio silently stared at the young woman as she grew smaller in the distance. When he could no longer see her he opened his hand, and beheld her presence forever in a flower.

The War
Healer

1

He set himself in the middle of the battle-ground, between the two fighting factions. And there, with bullets whistling past, he patched up the wounded and buried the dead.

He had been a photographer, an on-looker, in a war-torn region. And one day, overcome by frustration at being so powerless to stop the fighting, he underwent an obscure conversion. He gave up his job, and became a sort of healer and burier of the dead.

It was bloody work indeed. He laboured alone. He performed this solitary unacknowl-edged task for years. He would wake up in the morning and go to the battleground and set about his grim blood-soaked work. He would arrive in a clean white shirt at dawn, and he would be blood-spattered by noon, and by the evening his glasses would be steamed over with blood and gore. His hands would be dripping with fat and the messy tissues of the dead and those hopelessly shot to pieces. He worked at healing and burying all day, in that hot place, in that no-man's land, in the desert, between two implacable enemies. It was a wonder he wasn't killed.

From day to day he survived all the shooting, bombing and shelling. No one joined him there. He was not paid for his work. No international organisations softened his task or knew what he did there alone. None of the warring sides knew what he did there either, what services he rendered so tirelessly, burying their dead, patching up their wounded.

2

Then one day he decided he needed to get married, and he took himself a wife. She was a good woman. His one wish was that he wouldn't have to work on their wedding day. So he chose a holy day when he hoped there would be no fighting; a day holy to both sides.

The day arrived. They were in their finest apparel. His wife was beautiful in her white wedding dress. He was simple in his black suit. But he was quite heart-broken when, on the day, the enemies struck up the fighting again, like an infernal orchestra. He had to leave the wedding service and hurry to the middle place in the fighting zone, and heal the wounded and bury the dead.

On this day his wife joined him. She was a sad vision in her bridal dress, her white bridal gown, and her white gloves. Together they worked very hard in the war zone, till her white nuptial attire had turned all bloody and darkened with gore, mud, blasted brains and intestines spewed up from all the shelling.

By the evening they were quite a sight in their filthy wedding outfits. They were shattered by the betrayal of the holy day by the implacable enemies. And they never really recovered from the peculiar ferocity of the day's bloodshed.

They were so distraught that they were tempted never to return to the war zone again. But the day passed and they had become man and wife. She told him that he may as well continue his thankless job as no one else knew what horrors happened there in the middle place between the two warring enemies. No one else could render the important services that he did. It was a condition he had accepted, she said.

And so, with a broken heart, he continued to work there in the middle place. He buried the dead, fixed up the wounded, from dawn to dusk. But he was not so alone any more. It still remained a wonder he was never killed or hurt by all those bullets, all that bombing. This fact never occurred to him as he did his work, nor afterwards.

3

He carried on his grim vocation. The years passed. A child was born to him by his good wife. The world changed. But still the fight continued between the unforgiving enemies. He worked as long as the war raged. While they murdered one another, he restored, buried, healed.

In a world where no one listens, where no one seems to care, where hatred is greater than love, where hearts are hardened by vengeance and pride, where violence is preferable to peace, what else is there for him to do but heal the wounded, and bury the dead, in a war that could go on forever?

The
Message

1

You arrive dirty and hungry. You are covered in grime. You have come from beyond the snowline. It has been an epic journey.

You have travelled through forests, through innumerable cities and villages, barely stopping, travelling mostly on foot, with no change of clothes.

You have come through regions where you were unfamiliar with the language and the customs. You have slept at roadsides, in strange inns. You have travelled alone, bearing a message which only you can carry.

How long have you been travelling? You don't know. Maybe your whole life.

You forego pleasures on the way. It's been hard enough just keeping on the journey. You have travelled nights without sleeping, days without eating. Your destination is your rest and your food. Your mission is to arrive at the court, deliver the message, and then to be free.

Many countries you have crossed, wolves you have battled, hard men you have trans-cended, cunning men you have eluded, seducing women you have slithered away from.

Youth deserted you in the virgin forests; and yet you travelled with youth, and never lost it. Youth remains in you, in your freedom and the simplicity of your spirit. Encased in the dirt of the road is your preserved freshness.

2

The last part of the journey was the worst. Getting closer was also getting farther. It is easier to get lost within sight of the palace. It is easier to feel one has arrived when one sees the battlements and turrets, the flags and banners of the castle. Then in renewed hope and exultation one hurries. And yet the way is still far. Distances are deceptive. Hope makes all things near, and so can prove treacherous.

You kept your eyes on the road. You nearly got lost in the village. You were tempted to stay the night, to divulge your destination to an old woman, and thus be given conflicting or self-serving advice. But you kept it to yourself. You imagined you were still at the beginning of your journey. You were conscious that it was still full of perils, and that you still had a long way to go.

Your whole life had been the journey. If you stopped to think now, or confess despair, who knows what snares of your own making you would fall into. So you staked your life on the journey. The journey was your life, your life on the road. You might have died on it, but you were vigilant. You took each moment as the whole. That's what you did.

3

And then you found you had arrived. You were in the court. You were in the place. In the grime and dirt of the journey the message was divested of you. It was painless. You didn't even know what it was. The message was on you. The message was in your dirt, on your unwashed body, in your weary but alive spirit. The message was in your eyes. It was in your arrival, in your dreams, in your memory. It was in all you had brought, and the nothing that you had brought.

The message was divested of you. It was shorn off you, and you were light. You were cleaned up of your message. You were scrubbed and shaved of it, bathed and washed of it. The filthy clothes were taken off you, and you were given new ones that shone like light.

4

There had been a mysterious ceremony acknowledging the heroic nature of your journey. But the true gift of it was in your spirit, your inner liberation. There was a new eternal light in you.

Fresh, young, and free, you wander the streets of the kingdom. You have the sense of being in a new world, a luminous world. You are living an enchanted life in the kingdom.

You had set out early and had arrived sooner than you thought. You have a whole new life ahead of you. And so here you are, a youth with a spirit of shining gold, rich beyond measure in the lightness of your being. Everything is before you. Your main quest and journey is over, because you had begun early and arrived early. Now you have it all to live, in peerless freedom. What luck! No need to fret, but just to live, now, the life you want.

Like a youth just arrived in a great city, with hope in his heart, looking to make his fortune and find his true love, in the happiest and most innocent days of his life, like such a youth you wander lightly through the streets of the mysterious kingdom. The pastel sky is touched with blue, and there is dawn sunlight.